WITCH DOCTOR

WITHDRAWN

**Written by
James Gelsey**

A
LITTLE APPLE
PAPERBACK

SCHOLASTIC INC.

New York Toronto London Auckland Sydney
Mexico City New Delhi Hong Kong Buenos Aires

For Max

ISBN 0-439-42075-X

Designed by Carisa Swenson

12 11 10 9 8 7 6 5 4 3 2 1   3 4 5 6 7 8/0

Special thanks to Duendes del Sur for cover and interior illustrations.
Printed in the U.S.A.
First printing, December 2003

Chapter 1

"Last one to the luau's a rotten pineapple!" Shaggy called as he and Scooby ran out of the hotel. The flowered leis around their necks waved in the breeze as they ran across the parking lot.

"Shaggy! Scooby!" Velma called. "Would you two come back here, please?"

Shaggy and Scooby spun around and ran back over to Fred, Velma, and Daphne.

"Take it easy, fellas," Fred said. "The luau's not until this evening."

"This evening?" Shaggy repeated. "What are we supposed to do all day in Hawaii? It's

1

not like back home, where we can hang out at Louie's Pizza Parlor or the malt shop."

Fred, Daphne, and Velma shook their heads in disbelief.

"Shaggy, my uncle didn't invite us to come to Hawaii with him just so we could hang out in a pizza place or a malt shop," Daphne said.

"Daphne's right," Velma said. "We should use our time here to explore Polynesian culture and the awesome beauty of these volcanic islands."

"After we check up on Horace Goodbine, like my uncle asked," Daphne added. Shaggy and Scooby looked at each other and sighed.

"Ro ruau?" Scooby asked.

"No luau," Shaggy answered.

"Don't worry, fellas, we're going some-place very exciting," Daphne said.

"Believe me, Daph, there's nothing as exciting as drinking punch from a coconut shell. Except for chowing down on barbecued yummies roasted over an open pit," Shaggy said.

"Oh, yeah?" asked Fred. "Then how about that?"

Fred pointed over Shaggy's right shoulder. Shaggy and Scooby turned and looked around the parking lot.

"You mean we're going to that blue SUV?" asked Shaggy.

"No, Shaggy, we're not going to that blue SUV," Velma said.

"Ruh red redan?" tried Scooby.

"We're not going to visit cars!" Velma replied in frustration. "Look up over the cars and tell us what you see."

Shaggy and Scooby focused their eyes on the area above and beyond the row of cars in the parking lot.

"I don't know, Velma," Shaggy said. "All I see are some palm trees."

"Rand ra rountain," Scooby added.

"That's no ordinary mountain," Fred said. "It's Mount Kumbaya."

"It's where Horace Goodbine has set up a small laboratory," Daphne continued.

"And . . . it's a volcano," Velma said.

Shaggy's and Scooby's eyes widened in surprise.

"Rolcano?" asked Scooby.

"As in, lava that's so hot it makes biting into a pizza and burning the roof of your mouth feel like eating a snow cone?" asked Shaggy.

"I guess you could say that." Daphne nodded.

"Rool," Scooby said with a smile.

"Cool?" Shaggy said. "You won't be saying that when the lava shoots out and melts you into a puddle of dog fur."

"Relax, Shaggy," Velma said. "Mount Kumbaya hasn't erupted in hundreds of years."

A honking interrupted their conversation. The gang watched as a minivan decorated like a giant pineapple drove around the hotel driveway.

"Rineapple," Scooby said, licking his lips.

"Man, is this island great or what?" Shaggy said. "Even the vans look like food. I'd like to meet the person who thought of that."

"You're about to," Fred said. "Because that's our ride."

The pineapple van stopped in front of the gang and the passenger window slid down.

"Aloha, friends," a woman called from inside the van. "Hop in!"

"There's no way you're getting me to ride in a giant pineapple to visit a dangerous volcano," Shaggy said.

"I didn't know if you ate breakfast yet," the woman called out. "So I brought along some homemade macadamia treats. I hope you don't mind."

Shaggy's eyes lit up. He pushed the others aside and jumped into the van.

"Well, what are we waiting for?" he asked. "Let's eat! I mean, let's go!"

Chapter 2

"I'm Terry Hawakami," the woman said. "Dr. Goodbine sent me to bring you to his private lab on the mountain."

"Don't you mean volcano?" asked Velma.

"Yes, I suppose so," Terry answered with a smile. She peered into the rearview mirror to check on Shaggy and Scooby. "How are those macadamia treats?"

Scooby stopped eating long enough to say, "Rummy!"

Terry steered the van onto a narrow road off the highway. Then she reached into a bag next to her seat and pulled out some strings with cards attached.

"Here, you all need to put these on," she said.

"What are they?" asked Fred.

"Security passes," Terry answered. "Every-one needs a pass to get onto the mountain road."

As she spoke, she stopped the van at a guardhouse. The guard came over and had Terry sign a clipboard.

"I see there are other visitors here already," Terry said.

The guard nodded without saying a word. Then he stepped back into the guardhouse and allowed the van to continue.

"Why such high security for a volcano that hasn't erupted for over three hundred years?" asked Daphne.

"Because Dr. Goodbine's research into extracting minerals from the volcanic soil is highly confidential," Terry answered. Then she quickly covered her mouth. "Oops, I shouldn't have said that."

"Don't worry, your secret is safe with us," Daphne said.

"I wish you could convince Dr. Goodbine of that," Terry said. "It's not the first time I've let something slip. That's why he has me driving the van instead of working in his lab. I'll do anything to get back to work there. I got my degree in geology to do just that kind of work." Her cheerful expression clouded over.

"Almost done with the cookies," Shaggy called. "Got anything else?"

"Sorry, that's all," Terry answered. "Next time I'll have to bring you my tiki crisps."

"Riki risp?" asked Scooby.

"Like, what's a tiki?" asked Shaggy. "One of those triangular houses that Native Americans used to live in?"

"No, Shaggy, those are tepees," Velma said. "Tikis are . . . well, there's one now."

The van passed a tall wooden statue on the side of the road.

"Zoinks!" Shaggy cried. "That's got to be one of the freakiest things I've ever seen!"

"Shaggy! That's not very nice," Daphne said.

"It's all right," Terry said. "He's right. They are kind of freaky-looking. They are statues of Polynesian gods. As we make our way up the mountain, you'll start seeing more of them. They are the guardians of Mount Kumbaya, but over time they've been slowly disappearing. Some of the locals say that just before the volcano erupts, the grand witch doctor will come to the mountain. When he does, he will turn the tikis into humans and any humans he finds into tiki statues."

Shaggy and Scooby put down their macadamia treats.

"You mean those statues will come to life?" asked Shaggy. "I think I've just lost my appetite."

"Ree roo," Scooby echoed, putting his snack down.

"Have the volcanologists confirmed that Mount Kumbaya will erupt?" asked Velma.

"Volcanologist?" Shaggy said. "You made that word up, right?"

"A volcanologist is a scientist who studies volcanoes," Fred said.

"No, the scientists can't find any reason to believe the volcano will erupt," Terry said. "All they found is an increase in the geyser activity along the mountain's south face."

As Terry steered the van around a sharp bend, the gang noticed more wooden tikis along the side of the road. Some were standing, and some had fallen over. But the statues' large faces, with deep-set eyes and open mouths, seemed a little eerie.

Around the next bend, Terry stopped the van beside a small white building.

"Here we are," she announced. "Dr. Goodbine's lab."

"Thanks for the ride, Terry," Daphne said.

As the gang got out of the van, they heard a cell phone ring. Terry answered it and had a brief conversation.

"That was Dr. Goodbine," she said, rolling her eyes. "He'll be right out. I wish I could stay, but he's sending me on an urgent mis-

sion. He needs more macadamia treats. I'll be
back later to get you."

The gang watched Terry drive back down
the road.

"What exactly is Dr. Goodbine working
on for your uncle, Daphne?" asked Velma.

But before Daphne could answer, a strange
voice said, "Something that will change the
world forever!"

Chapter 3

"Who're you?" Velma asked.

"Norman Sumpump," the man said, extending his hand. He looked down and realized his hand was filthy. He quickly withdrew it. "Sorry, I've been taking soil samples around here." He removed two small bottles filled with dirt from his vest pocket.

"How do you know what Dr. Goodbine is working on, Mr. Sumpump?" Fred asked.

"That's *Doctor* Sumpump to you," he replied. "Horace Goodbine and I once did some research together on the mineral-rich soils around volcanoes. I was away on an expedition when some wealthy philanthropist offered Horace the chance to run his own lab. Horace just packed up without telling me. When I came back, he was gone. I think that Horace discovered something big and didn't want me to be a part of it."

"Why don't you ask him?" asked Daphne.

Dr. Sumpump looked around and then leaned in toward the gang. "He doesn't know I'm here," he whispered. "I'm going to wait for just the right moment and then confront him." As Dr. Sumpump spoke, he noticed something shining on the ground. He picked it up and examined it closely.

"Now what's this doing here?" he said to himself.

"What is it, Dr. Sumpump?" Velma asked.

"It's a gemstone that has absolutely no business being on a mountain in Hawaii," he answered.

"Kinda like us, right, Scoob?" Shaggy whispered.

"Rou red rit!" Scooby barked.

Dr. Sumpump put the small vials of dirt back into one vest pocket and took a small magnifying glass out of another. He studied the stone more closely.

"This gemstone shares some properties  with the soil around here," he said. "But there aren't supposed to be any gems like this on the mountain. I wonder . . ."

Dr. Sumpump's eyes narrowed in deep thought. A sudden series of clicking sounds coming from the lab snapped him out of it.

"He's coming!" Dr. Sumpump said. "Not a word about my being here." Dr. Sumpump dashed off down a path leading behind the lab.

The clicking sounds stopped, and the lab

door creaked open. A tall figure stood in the shadow of the doorway.

"Pssssst!" the stranger called. A tall, youngish-looking man with red hair and a long white lab coat stepped out into the sunlight. He motioned to the gang to enter the building.

The gang followed the man through the doorway and into a small outer room. The door behind them closed automatically. Once it slammed shut, the gang heard that series of clicks again.

"Automatic locks," the man said. "I'm Dr. Goodbine."

"I'm Daphne Blake, Dr. Goodbine, and these are my friends," Daphne said.

Horace Goodbine eyed the rest of the gang warily.

"My uncle said you'd be able to show us around your lab," she continued.

"My lab?" Horace said nervously.

"We were hoping you could show us some of the things you're working on for Daphne's uncle," Velma said. "Personally, I'm very interested in learning more about your research on mineral-enriched soils."

Horace's eyes widened in surprise.

"Oh, so you, uh, know about my research," he said. "Let me guess. Terry told you."

"She, uh, did mention something about extracting minerals from the soil," Fred said.

Horace Goodbine nodded. "And then I turn the minerals into gems," he added. "Not very big or valuable, mind you, but gems all the same."

"So does that mean we can see the lab?" Velma asked.

"Oh, the lab," Horace said. "I don't think so. It's a bit of a mess right now."

"Oh, well, can't see the lab," Shaggy said. "You know what that means, right, Scoob?"

"Rit's ruau rime!" Scooby announced. He and Shaggy did a little Hawaiian dance around the tiny room, bumping into everyone else.

"Knock it off, you two," Velma said.

"Isn't there anything you can show us?" Daphne asked.

Horace thought for a minute. "Wait right here," he said. Quick as a wink, he disappeared behind the door to the lab. A moment later, he reappeared. "Follow me."

"Where are we going?" asked Velma.

"To the top of the volcano!" Horace announced.

Chapter 4

The gang followed Horace Goodbine along a narrow path up Mount Kumbaya. As they rounded a bend, the path opened up onto a large, flat plain dotted with several tiki statues. Suddenly, one of the statues started to move.

"Zoinks!" Shaggy cried. "That tiki statue's alive! Let's get out of here before the witch doctor turns us into tiki statues!"

"That's not a tiki statue, Shaggy," Velma said. "It's a real live person."

"That used to be a tiki statue," Shaggy said.

"If you ask me, it seems a little suspicious that someone else would be all the way up here," Fred said.

"You're right, Fred," Daphne agreed. "I say we go see who it is."

The stranger turned out to be a woman. She was carefully filling glass vials with dirt. Her bright hair sparkled in the sunlight.

"Excuse us," Fred said, startling the woman. She dropped two of the vials, sending a plume of dust onto her pants.

"Now look what you've done," the woman said. "I've got dirt all over my new pants!" She took a tiny brush from her fanny pack and swept it over her pants, dusting off the dirt. "What are you kids doing here anyway? This is a restricted area."

"We know," Velma replied. She and the others held out their security tags. "We're here with Dr. Goodbine."

Horace regarded the woman for a moment. He noticed the security badge hanging off her fanny pack. Then he looked down at the vials of dirt.

"You know, ma'am, you're not allowed to remove soil from the mountain," Horace said. "You may have a security pass to be here, but you need the governor's approval to do any kind of research involving —"

The woman held up her left hand. With her right hand, she removed a tiny cell phone from her back pocket. She flipped open the mouthpiece and held the phone out to Horace. "It's speed dial three," she said.

"What is?" he asked.

"The governor," the woman answered.

"Are you a scientist, too?" Daphne asked.

"In a manner of speaking," the woman answered. "I'm Eudora Truffle, and I'm an expert on the science of beauty."

"I didn't know there was such a thing," Fred said.

"I came here to take dirt samples," Eudora said. "The mineral-rich soil around the volcano will be perfect for the mud baths at the new spa I'm opening at the bottom of the mountain."

"A spa?" Horace asked. "How did you ever get the governor to give you permission for that?"

Eudora Truffle smiled. "Tourism," she said. "My spa will attract tourists and beauty seekers from all over. It'll make Mount Kumbaya synonymous with beauty."

"But you'll use up all the dirt!" Horace exclaimed.

"So what?" Eudora replied.

"So, like, Dr. Goodbine needs the dirt for his —" Shaggy said before Daphne and Velma put their hands over his mouth.

Horace paled and clutched his backpack tightly.

"— his research," Daphne said quickly.

Eudora eyed Horace suspiciously. "Well, whatever," she said. "I came here to get dirt.

And I'm going to use that dirt to make Eudora's Magic Mud Spa the biggest thing in Hawaii. Now excuse me while I continue my work."

Eudora carefully picked up the last vial of dirt and dropped it into her fanny pack. Then she walked across the plain and disappeared down the path.

"Shaggy, that was very careless of you," Daphne said.

"Like, what'd I do?" Shaggy asked.

"You almost gave away Dr. Goodbine's secret," Fred said. "About how he's found a way to turn the soil around the volcano into gems."

"But there's not going to be any soil, much less gems, if that Truffle woman gets her way," Dr. Goodbine said. "We'd better go back to the lab so I can call —"

A loud scream pierced the air, interrupting Horace.

"Rikes!" Scooby cried, jumping into Shaggy's arms.

"What was that?" asked Daphne.

"It sounds like it's coming from the geyser field," Horace said. "Follow me!"

Chapter 5

The gang followed Horace to a clearing dotted with small craters. They heard the scream again and spun around. A burst of steam, water, and mud shot out of one of the craters and up into the air.

"Jeepers!" Daphne said. "Look at that!"

"It's a geyser," Horace said. "This side of the mountain is covered with them. That's why the volcano hasn't erupted in such a long time. All the pressure that builds up inside is released through the geysers."

"So that's what made that screaming noise," Velma said. "Fascinating."

"Whew!" Shaggy said. "I don't know about the rest of you, but I'm just glad it wasn't one of those tiki things."

"Those tiki things are just statues, Shaggy," Velma said. "And statues can't scream or run around or chase you off the mountain."

"But a witch doctor can!" Shaggy cried.

He pointed to a figure standing at the far end of the geyser field. It wore a long robe and a freaky mask with slits for the eyes and mouth.

"Ritch roctor!" Scooby yelled.

The creature ran right toward them, shouting, "Mulaba haga fofina!"

"Jinkies!" Velma cried. "It *is* a witch doctor!"

"Quick, before he turns us into statues!" Shaggy cried.

The witch doctor ran and waved a long stick with a skull mounted on the top. Then he grabbed the stick like a knight about to joust and ran directly at Horace Goodbine.

"Oh, no!" Horace cried, shutting his eyes tight.

In a swift, single motion, the witch doctor slid the tip of the pole through one of the straps on Horace's backpack. The scoundrel thrust the pole up, launching the backpack off Horace's back and into the air. The pack fell right into the witch doctor's hands.

"My backpack!" Horace yelled.

The witch doctor shouted something else in his strange language, then ran off through the geyser field.

"You've got to stop him!" Horace said. "My laptop's in the backpack. It's got all of my notes on the secret process!"

"Come on, gang!" Fred shouted. He and the others were starting across the field when one of the geysers suddenly erupted. Everyone stopped short as steam and mud shot into the sky.

"What's on the other side of the geyser field, Dr. Goodbine?" asked Fred.

"A place where they used to carve the tiki statues and have special ceremonies," Horace answered. "And just below that is the lab."

Fred thought for a minute. "Okay, gang, here's what we have to do," he said. "That old statuary sounds like a good place for a villain to hide, so Daphne and I will check it out."

"Good idea, Fred," said Velma. "Shaggy, Scooby, and I will continue to the other side of the statuary to see if the witch doctor went down to the lab."

"What about me?" asked Dr. Goodbine.

"Take the main path back to the lab, Dr.

Goodbine," Fred answered. "You may not find any clues, but you might run into someone who has seen the witch doctor."

"Someone like Eudora Truffle or Dr. Sumpump," Daphne added.

"Did you say Dr. Sumpump?" asked Horace.

"We ran into him earlier today outside your lab," Velma said. "Just before you came out."

"I wonder what he's doing here," Horace said.

"He said something about being your research partner and that you went behind his back to get the grant from my uncle," Daphne said. "Is all that true?"

"Only the part about him once being my research partner," Horace said. "He went off on a three-month expedition. Then your uncle came and offered me the lab here. I tried for three weeks but couldn't reach Dr. Sumpump anywhere. I couldn't wait any longer. But I'm glad he's finally here."

"Judging by how angry he sounded, you may not be so glad," Velma said.

"One more reason not to waste any more time," Fred said. "To the clues!"

Chapter 6

"Come on, Shaggy," Velma said. "You too, Scooby. We've got to try to follow the witch doctor's trail before he can get away with Dr. Goodbine's laptop."

Velma led Shaggy and Scooby through the geyser field and down a dusty path into the statuary. There were piles of half-finished and broken tiki statues everywhere.

"This place gives me the heebie-jeebies," Shaggy said. "Or should I say the tiki-jeekies?"

Scooby chuckled as they walked farther into the sacred area.

"Look, Velma, a barbecue pit!" Shaggy announced, pointing to a large crater in the ground. "Maybe this is where they had their tiki luaus."

Velma studied the pit as they walked past. "I don't think you're that far off, Shaggy. My guess is that the witch doctor used this pit to make fires for his ceremonies."

They reached the far end of the statuary and looked down the slope at the lab.

"Well, there's Dr. Goodbine's lab," Velma said. "Now keep your eyes peeled for any signs of the monster's trail."

"What kind of trail would a witch doctor leave behind?" Shaggy asked.

"I don't know, Shaggy, but I'd settle for anything that shows us which way he went," Velma replied.

"Rike a rerurity rag?" Scooby said, pointing to a tag lying in the dirt.

"Now why would a witch doctor need a security tag?" Velma asked as she picked up the clue.

"To get permission to come up here and scare us to pieces," Shaggy said.

"Precisely," Velma said. "Only I don't think a real witch doctor would bother getting one. I'm going to show this to Fred and Velma. You two keep looking for other clues. Great job, Scooby."

"Ranks!" Scooby barked.

Velma went to find Fred and Daphne, leaving Shaggy and Scooby alone.

"Good work, Scooby," Shaggy said. "Now we're one step closer to Luau City." He and Scooby started their little Hawaiian dance again.

"Let's see if we can dance our way down to the lab," Shaggy said.

The two of them wiggled their hips and waved their arms down the path.

"Hey, we're getting pretty good at this," Shaggy said.

Suddenly, the sound of a drumbeat filled the air.

"Hey, we've got some accompaniment!" Shaggy said. The rhythmic beat of the drum matched Shaggy and Scooby's dance.

"Ris is run!" Scooby said.

"Sure is," Shaggy agreed. "But I wonder where the drum is coming from?"

The drumbeats got louder. Shaggy and Scooby spun around and saw the witch doctor playing a tall drum.

"Zoinks!" Shaggy screamed. "It's a musical monster!"

The witch doctor shouted at Shaggy and Scooby in his strange language. Then he threw down the drum and waved his arms angrily.

"For our last dance, Scooby, let's boogie out of here!" Shaggy shouted.

Shaggy and Scooby ran the rest of the way to the lab building. The witch doctor chased after them, shouting and waving his stick. Shaggy and Scooby raced around to the front of the building and jumped inside.

They slammed the door but could still hear the witch doctor's shouts outside.

"Come on, Scooby, we don't have much time," Shaggy said. They tried opening the inner door to the lab but found it locked. He and Scooby pulled and pounded on the door as hard as they could. Just as they were giving up hope, something tapped them on the shoulder.

"Rikes!" Scooby cried, jumping into Shaggy's arms.

"Zoinks!" Shaggy shouted.

"Ahhhhh!" screamed a strange voice.

$\mathcal{S}$haggy and Scooby opened their eyes and saw Dr. Goodbine standing in the hallway. His eyes were tightly shut and his face was scrunched up into a grimace.

"Dr. Goodbine?" Shaggy said. "Like, is that you?"

Horace Goodbine opened one eye, then the other.

"Oh, Shaggy, Scooby, you two startled me," he said. "Are you all right?"

"That witch doctor chased us in here," Shaggy said. "We tried to get inside the lab, but there were too many locks on the door."

Just then, Fred, Daphne, and Velma peered inside.

"Is everything all right?" Fred asked.

"The witch doctor almost got into the lab," Dr. Goodbine said.

"That's good news," Daphne said.

Dr. Goodbine looked surprised.

"Because that way we know the witch doctor is still around," Velma explained. "Did you see anyone on your way down here, Dr. Goodbine?"

Dr. Goodbine shook his head. "What about you?" he asked.

"No, but we did find some clues," Fred said. "Velma, Shaggy, and Scooby found this security pass on the path up the hill."

"And then we found this vial of dirt in the statuary," Daphne said.

"This witch doctor seems to be very careless," Dr. Goodbine said. "Leaving all these clues around, I mean."

"It does seem strange," Daphne said.

"But maybe all it really cares about is your laptop."

"And we'd better find more clues fast if we're going to get it back," Velma said.

"Well, I don't know about the rest of you," Shaggy said, "but Scooby and I have had enough fun for one day. We're ready to call it quits and go back to the hotel."

"No one's going anywhere until we solve this mystery, Shaggy," Fred said.

"Besides, how are you and Scooby going to get back to the hotel?" asked Daphne. "It's miles away, and you two haven't even eaten lunch yet."

"Don't remind us," Shaggy said. "But we'll be back there luauing to our hearts' content before you know it. Hit it, Scoob. Call us a cab."

Scooby took a tiny cell phone out from under his collar. He flipped open the mouthpiece. "Rhat's ruh rumber?" he asked.

Shaggy snapped his fingers in disappointment. "Man! I knew we forgot something," he moaned.

Fred, Daphne, and Velma stared at the cell phone.

"Scooby, where did you get that?" Velma asked.

"Ris?" He held out the cell phone. "Routside."

"Where outside?" asked Fred.

"I dunno," Shaggy said. "We were dancing our way down the mountain when the witch doctor started chasing us. He must have dropped it, because we found it on the ground just before we ran in here."

Fred, Velma, and Daphne nodded at one another.

"That's it!" Fred said.

"That's what?" asked Dr. Goodbine.

"The last clue," Daphne said.

"Really? Mystery solved? Time for the luau!" Shaggy sang.

"Not so fast, Shaggy," Velma said. "There's one more thing we have to do before we can go." Shaggy and Scooby hung their heads. "We know," they sighed.

"Rime ro ret a rap," Scooby said.

Dr. Goodbine tried to make out what Scooby had said, but couldn't quite get it.

"What was that Scooby said?" he asked.

"Time to set a trap," Fred said. "The fact that the witch doctor chased Shaggy and

Scooby to the lab tells me there's something else he wants."

"But what?" asked Daphne.

"Maybe the specially designed sifting and sorting apparatus I designed," Dr. Goodbine said. "The process itself is useless without it."

"And so is our trap," Fred said. "Listen up, everyone."

Chapter 8

"Dr. Goodbine, can you unlock the door to the lab so we can lure the witch doctor inside?" Fred asked.

"I don't know, Fred," Dr. Goodbine said. "There's a lot of expensive equipment in there."

"I'll help you put those things away," Velma said. "That way, you won't have to worry about Shaggy and Scooby breaking anything."

"Like, excuse me, but why would Scooby and I be in there breaking anything?" asked Shaggy.

"Because you two are going to be pretending to use Dr. Goodbine's apparatus," Fred said. "And when the witch doctor shows up, you'll grab it and run out of the lab."

"The witch doctor will chase you up the hill to the statuary, where we'll be waiting," Daphne said.

"All you have to do is get the witch doctor to the big pit in the middle," Fred said. "We'll have it covered so when the witch doctor runs over it, he'll fall inside."

"Sounds like a good plan, Fred, except for one thing," Shaggy said. "That part where the crazy witch doctor chases me and Scooby will never work."

"Why not?" asked Daphne.

"'Cause we won't be here!" Shaggy said. "Let's go, Scoob. I'll bet if we start walking now, we'll be back to the hotel just in time for the luau."

"Not so fast, you two," Velma said. "Dr. Goodbine really needs our help, and that includes you. So how about it, Scooby? Will you do it for a Scooby Snack?"

"Rooby rack? Rummy!" Scooby nodded. Daphne tossed four Scooby Snacks into the air. Scooby stuck out his tongue and waited for the treats to land right in the middle of it. Then he slurped his tongue back into his mouth, munching up the snacks.

"Now let's get started," Fred said.

Fred and Daphne went back up to the statuary to cover the pit. Dr. Goodbine unlocked the lab door. He and Velma went inside to put things away.

"Do we really have to use the apparatus?" asked Dr. Goodbine. "I just don't want anything to happen to it."

Velma thought for a moment. "Has anyone else ever seen it?" she asked.

"No, it's my own special design," Dr. Goodbine answered.

"Then let's put it away and use something else," Velma said. "Unless the witch doctor has a degree in chemistry, I don't think he'll know the difference. Shaggy, Scooby, you two put on these lab coats."

Shaggy and Scooby took their positions behind a long table filled with all kinds of lab equipment.

"Come on, Dr. Goodbine, let's go down to the guardhouse and let them know what's going on," Velma said. "Shaggy and Scooby have everything under control here."

"They do?" asked Dr. Goodbine.

"Oh, sure," Shaggy said. "We've got lots of practice getting chased by monsters."

Soon, the two of them were alone.

"Well, Scooby, what should we do first?" asked Shaggy. "Should we discombobulate the funkelator? Or mix the higgledipum with the flibbetyfloob?"

The two of them started laughing, so they didn't hear the footsteps in the hallway. Before they knew what was happening, the witch doctor burst into the lab.

"Mulaba fofina haga! Clee clee!" the witch doctor shouted as he lunged at the lab table.

"Quick, Scoob, grab the multiplexmodulator!" Shaggy cried.

"Rhat?" Scooby asked.

"The thingamajig! Grab the thingamajig and run!" Shaggy replied.

Scooby grabbed something off the lab table and ran out the door with Shaggy right in front of him.

"Up the hill to the statuary, Scoob!" Shaggy shouted. The two of them ran, with the witch doctor in pursuit. He waved his long, skull-tipped pole and continued shouting in his strange language.

The two of them ran into the statuary and headed right for the hidden pit. They saw Fred and Daphne crouched down behind a large tiki statue. Scooby jumped through the air over the covered pit. Shaggy started to jump but lost his balance and tripped.

"Look out below!" he shouted as he fell through the covering of palm leaves and into the pit.

The witch doctor saw Shaggy fall and ran around the pit after Scooby. Scooby quickly realized the witch doctor was still on his tail. So he sped up and raced toward the geyser field. The witch doctor got closer and almost grabbed Scooby's tail! Scooby was so startled, he accidentally dropped the apparatus.

The witch doctor tried to grab it, but he tripped over a fallen tiki statue! The monster stumbled into a crater. A moment later, the ground rumbled and a burst of steam, water,

and mud sent the witch doctor shooting
straight up into the sky!

"Help! Help!" he screamed.

"Sounds like our monster speaks more
than tiki-ese," Daphne said, shaking her head.

Chapter 9

The witch doctor lay on the ground, moaning in pain.

"Ohhhh, my back," he groaned. The witch doctor sat up and looked at the dirt and mud covering his body. "My legs. My arms. My everything. I'm filthy!"

Dr. Goodbine and Velma drove up in a Jeep with two security guards.

"Did you catch him?" asked Dr. Goodbine.

"Here he is," Fred said. "Would you like to see who's really behind this tiki mystery?"

"Without question," Dr. Goodbine said.

He reached over and tugged at the witch doctor's head. The large mask came off in Dr. Goodbine's hand.

"Eudora Truffle!" Dr. Goodbine exclaimed.

"Just as we suspected," Daphne said.

"You did? How on earth did you know?" asked Dr. Goodbine.

"It wasn't easy," Velma said. "At first, we had a few suspects in mind. And when we found the security pass, we realized it had to be someone who came up to Mount Kumbaya today."

"Like Dr. Sumpump, Ms. Truffle, or Terry Hawakami," Fred said. "They all seemed to have reasons for wanting to get back at Dr. Goodbine."

Dr. Goodbine nodded thoughtfully as the gang continued.

"Then we found that vial of dirt in the statuary," Fred said. "And we remembered that both Dr. Sumpump and Ms. Truffle were taking soil samples for different reasons."

Dr. Goodbine smiled. "Of course, so that eliminated Terry Hawakami from suspicion," he said.

"That's what we thought, too," Daphne said. "But then Scooby found this last clue outside the lab." She held up the cell phone. "And we remembered that Terry had one just like it with her in the van."

"So she was still a suspect?" asked Dr. Goodbine, his smile turning into a frown of confusion.

"Not really," Velma continued. "Because we remembered that Ms. Truffle also had a cell phone. She dared you to call the governor on it, remember?"

"We even checked out speed dial three,"

Fred said. "Turned out to be the phone number of the department store where Ms. Truffle works in the cosmetics department."

"So Eudora Truffle was the only suspect who matched up with all three clues," Velma concluded. "They kept falling out of her fanny pack, which she wore under her costume. By the way, it looks like she got what she was after."

"How so?" Dr. Goodbine said.

"She gets to be the first person to test the power of Eudora's Magic Mud," Daphne said, smiling.

"And she'll have plenty of time to see how well it works," one of the guards said. "Let's go, Ms. Truffle."

"I was so close," Eudora said as the guards pulled her to

her feet. "I was going to use that special process of yours to literally turn my beauty spa into a gold mine. I had the laptop and I was *this close* to getting your special equipment when those kids and their pesky pooch ruined everything."

"Where is my laptop?" asked Dr. Good-bine anxiously.

"Hidden inside the tiki statue closest to the lab," she said as the guards put her in their Jeep. "Hey, what are you doing? Let go of me! I know the governor!"

Terry pulled up in the van as the Jeep drove away.

"What's going on?" she asked.

"You wouldn't believe it if we told you," Fred said.

"Hop in and try me," she said with a smile.

Everyone got into the van. They stopped on the way down the mountain so Dr. Good-bine could lock up his lab. Then they told Terry the entire story.

Dr. Goodbine said, "I just wish I could think of a way to thank you kids, and especially Scooby-Doo."

Terry thought for a moment, then took out her cell phone and had a quiet conversation with someone.

That night, Dr. Goodbine brought the gang to their first authentic Hawaiian luau. Shaggy and Scooby danced around in grass skirts. Terry stood up and signaled Dr. Goodbine, who joined her around the fire.

"May we have your attention, please?" Terry called.

All the activity stopped as Dr. Goodbine stepped forward.

"In appreciation for helping save the mountain, we have the honor of presenting Mount Kumbaya's newest guardian," he announced.

Terry and Dr. Goodbine lifted a sheet off a giant statue. The crowd burst into laughter and applause for the Scooby-Doo tiki statue before them.

"Hey, look at that, Scoob," Shaggy said. "You've been tiki-fied!"

"Scooby-Dooby-Doo!" cheered Scooby.

MOO
WAS
HERE